LOOK AROUND!
A Book About Shapes

LOOK AROUND!

A Book About Shapes

BY LEONARD EVERETT FISHER

Viking Kestrel

The artwork was painted with acrylics on textured paper.

VIKING KESTREL
Viking Penguin Inc., 40 West 23rd Street, New York, New York 10010, U.S.A.
Penguin Books Ltd, Harmondsworth, Middlesex, England
Penguin Books Australia Ltd, Ringwood, Victoria, Austrailia
Penguin Books Canada Limited, 2801 John Street, Markham, Ontario, Canada L3R 1B4
Penguin Books (N.Z.) Ltd, 182–190 Wairau Road, Auckland 10, New Zealand

First published in 1987 by Viking Penguin Inc.
Published simultaneously in Canada
Printed in Japan by Dai Nippon Printing Co. Ltd.
Set in Bembo
1 2 3 4 5 90 89 88 87

Library of Congress Cataloging in Publication Data
Fisher, Leonard Everett.   Look around.
Summary: Presents basic shapes in familiar scenes for the reader to identify.
1. Geometry—Juvenile literature.   [1. Shape] I. Title.   QA447.F5 1987   516'.15   86-40367   ISBN 0-670-80869-5

For Elizabeth and Susan

CIRCLE

A circle is a round shape.
It has no beginning.
It has no end.
The center is always as
far from one edge of
the circle as it is
from another.

Can you find these shapes on the next page?

Which shape is not a circle?

SQUARE

A square has four
straight sides.
All the sides are the
same size.

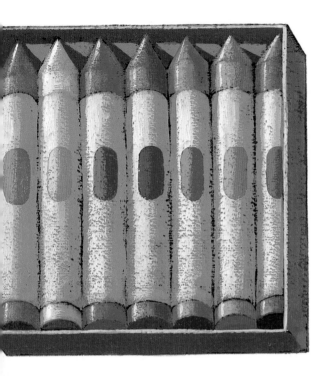

/ The Bright School
Chattanooga, Tennessee

Can you find these shapes on the next page?

Are all the shapes squares?

RECTANGLE

A rectangle has four straight sides.
The top and bottom are one size.
The left and right sides are another size.

Can you find these shapes on the next page?

Which ones are not rectangles?

TRIANGLE

A triangle has three straight sides. Sometimes the sides are the same size. Sometimes they are not.

Can you find these shapes on the next page?

Are they all triangles?

LOOK AROUND!

Can you find things that are a

or a  , a , or a  ?

A  has squares all over it.

 are rectangles with squares and circles.

A  wears a  in the shape of a triangle.

A  is made up of circles and a triangle.

A STOP is an octagon.

And a  is shaped like a heart.

LOOK AROUND!

More Shapes

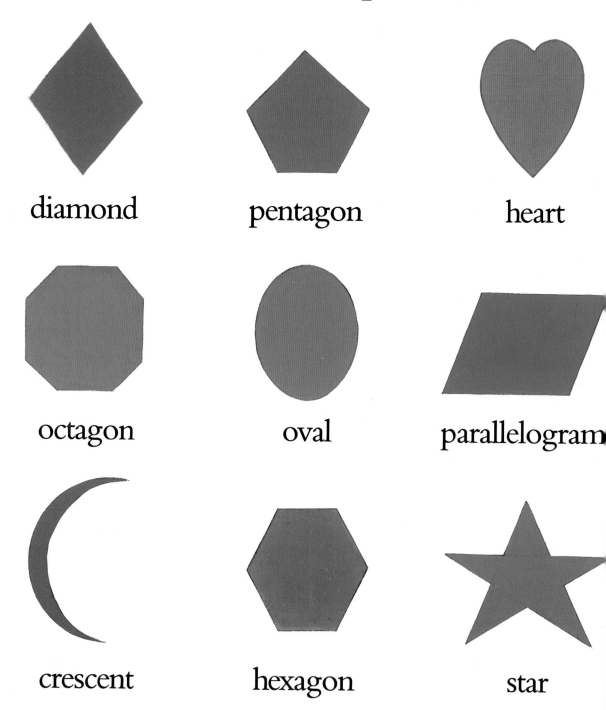

diamond

pentagon

heart

octagon

oval

parallelogram

crescent

hexagon

star

DATE DUE

GAYLORD | | | PRINTED IN U.S.A